I0796640

Animal
Groups
All About
Animals
Maria Koran
EYEDISCOVER

Go to www.eyediscover.com and enter this book's unique code.

BOOK CODE

AVM36925

EYEDISCOVER brings you optic readalongs that support active learning.

Published by AV² by Weigl
350 5th Avenue, 59th Floor New York, NY 10118
Website: www.eyediscover.com

Library of Congress Cataloging-in-Publication Data
available on request

ISBN 978-1-7911-0742-0 (hardcover)

Printed in Guangzhou, China
1 2 3 4 5 6 7 8 9 0 23 22 21 20 19

072019
121818

Project Coordinator: John Willis
Designer: Mandy Christiansen and Ana María Vidal

Weigl acknowledges Alamy, Getty Images, iStock, and Minden Pictures as the primary image suppliers for this title.

EYEDISCOVER provides enriched content, optimized for tablet use, that supplements and complements this book. EYEDISCOVER books strive to create inspired learning and engage young minds in a total learning experience.

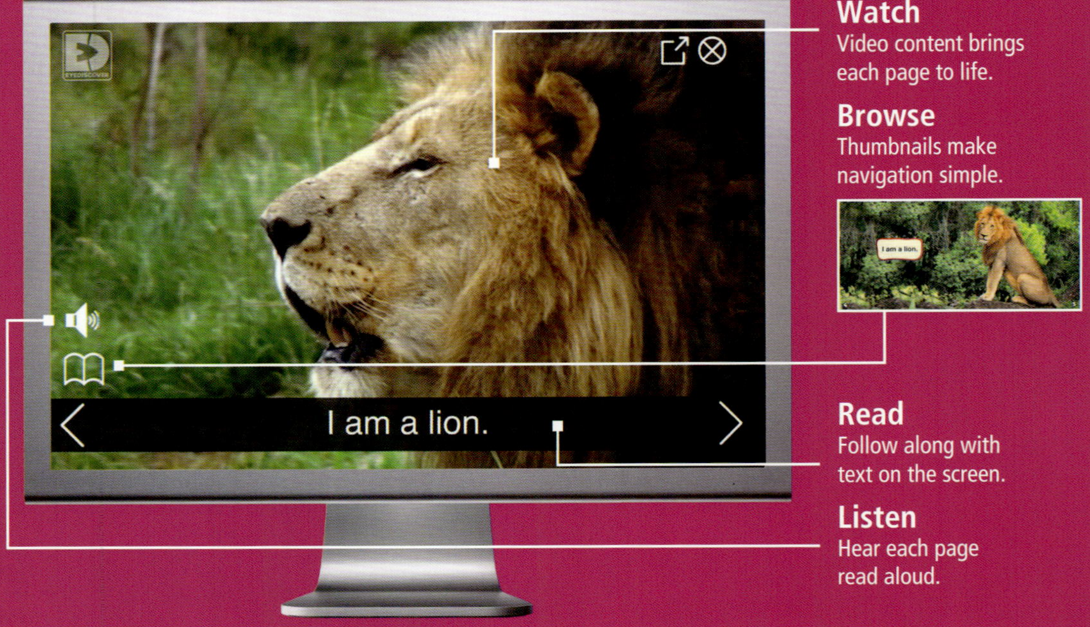

Your EYEDISCOVER Optic Readalongs come alive with...

Audio
Listen to the entire book read aloud.

Video
High resolution videos turn each spread into an optic readalong.

OPTIMIZED FOR

- TABLETS
- WHITEBOARDS
- COMPUTERS
- AND MUCH MORE!

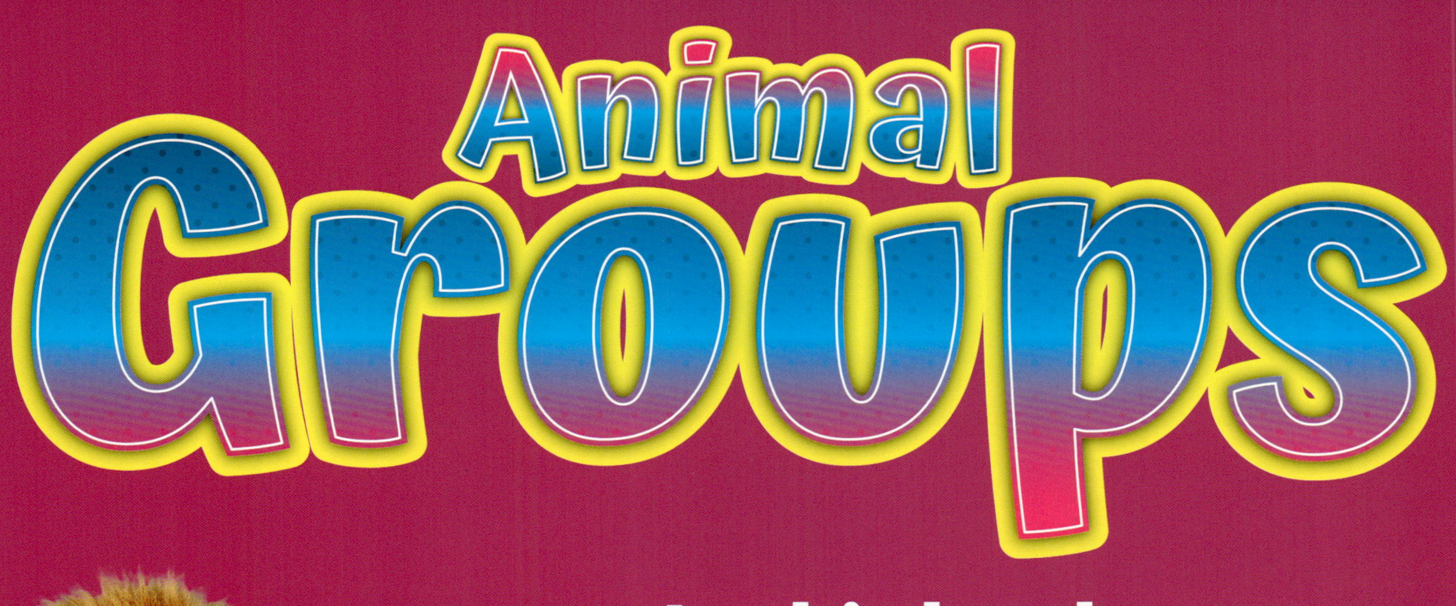

In this book, you will learn about

- what they are called
- what they are for

and much more!

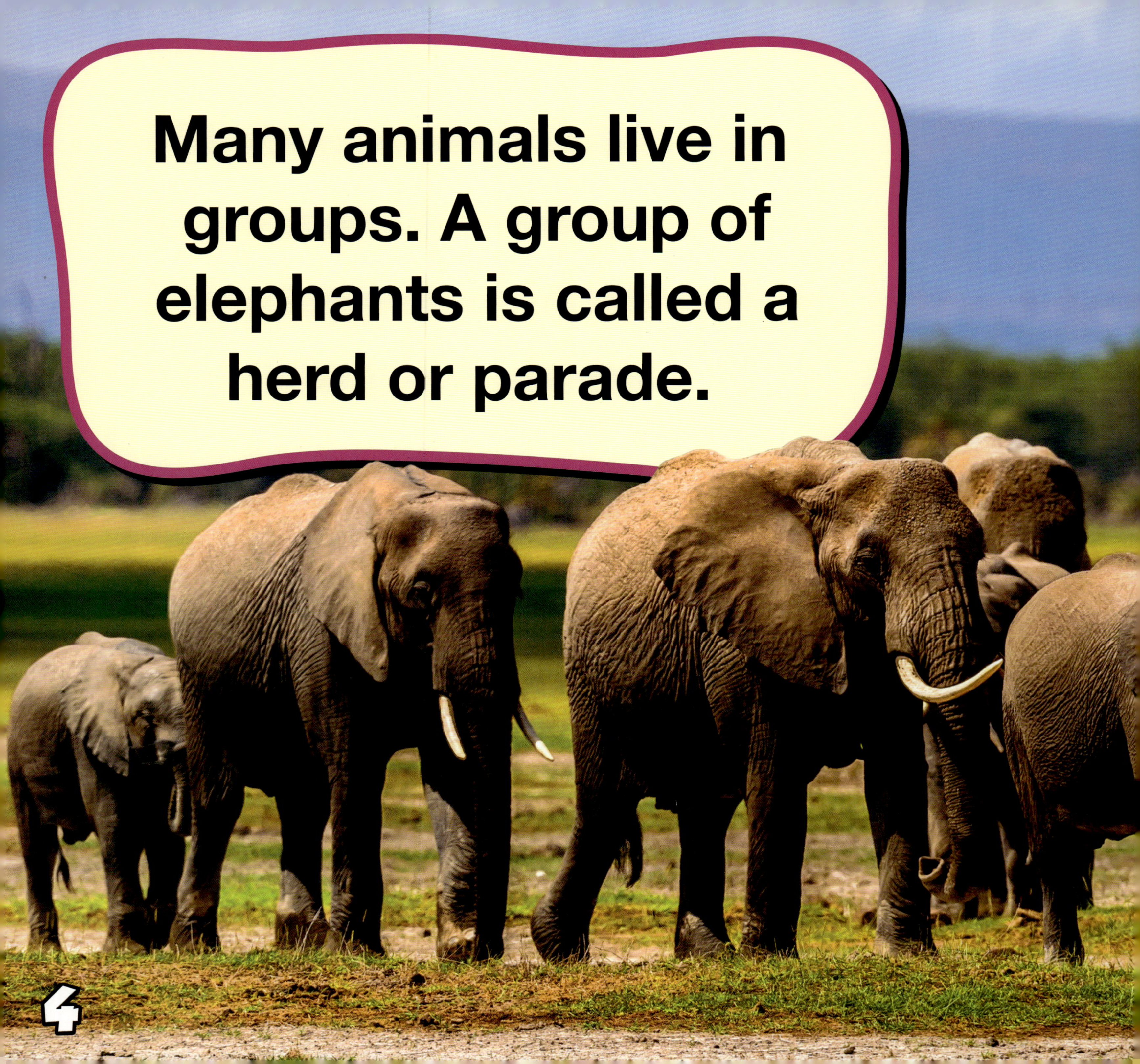

Many animals live in groups. A group of elephants is called a herd or parade.

Wolves live in packs. They help each other hunt for food.

Many whales live together in groups called pods. They talk to each other by singing.

Lions live and hunt in groups called prides.

Almost all monkeys live in groups. A group of monkeys is called a troop.

Many birds fly to new homes in winter. Ducks travel in groups called flocks.

A group of bats may sleep in a cave. This is called a colony.

Bees move in groups called swarms to find new homes.

Many fish swim in groups called schools. This helps keep them safe.

ANIMAL GROUPS BY THE NUMBERS

Herring can swim in **schools** of more than **4 billion** fish.

Most **wolves** live in **packs** of 6 to 10 animals.

A **pride** can have more than **30 lions**.

Mallard duck flocks may travel more than **700 miles** each spring and fall. (1,100 kilometers)

A **bee swarm** can have up to **30,000** insects.

The world's **largest bat colony** is in Bracken Cave in Texas. It has more than **15 million** bats.

KEY WORDS

Research has shown that as much as 65 percent of all written material published in English is made up of 300 words. These 300 words cannot be taught using pictures or learned by sounding them out. They must be recognized by sight. This book contains 31 common sight words to help young readers improve their reading fluency and comprehension. This book also teaches young readers several important content words, such as proper nouns. These words are paired with pictures to aid in learning and improve understanding.

Page	Sight Words First Appearance
4	a, animals, groups, in, is, live, many, of, or
7	each, food, for, help, other, they
8	by, talk, to, together
11	and
12	all, almost
15	homes, new
16	may, this
19	find, move
21	keep, schools, them

Page	Content Words First Appearance
4	elephants, herd, parade
7	packs, wolves
8	pods, whales
11	lions, prides
12	monkeys, troop
15	birds, ducks, flocks, winter
16	bats, cave, colony
19	bees, swarms
21	fish

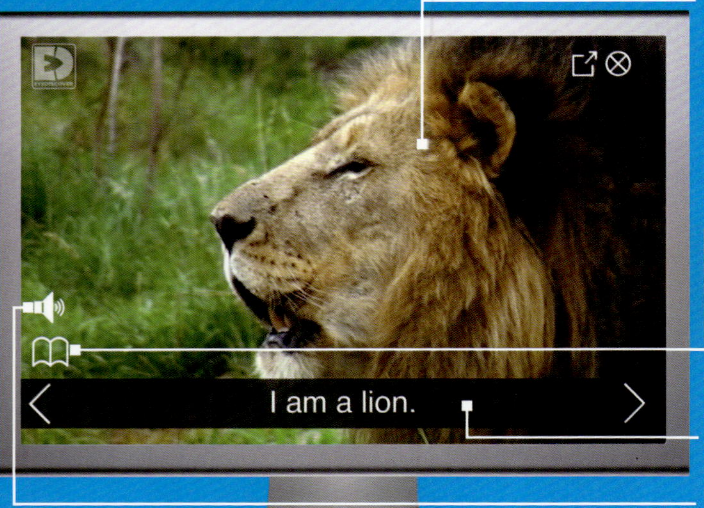

Watch
Video content brings each page to life.

Browse
Thumbnails make navigation simple.

Read
Follow along with text on the screen.

Listen
Hear each page read aloud.

Go to www.eyediscover.com and enter this book's unique code.

BOOK CODE

AVM36925